Captain Hook:

Villain or Victim?

Ellwyn Autumn

This story is based solely on the characters in the Peter Pan novel written by J.M. Barrie.

For Lost Kids Everywhere

Chapter 1

From the journal of David J. Locke:

Would you believe me if I told you that I met the most notorious pirate who ever lived? The scallywag of all scallywags—the only buccaneer Blackbeard himself feared? And that I survived to tell the tale?

If you don't believe me, listen to my story and let's see if I can convince you of its veracity. Even if you do not believe me, you must listen to the tale, for I'm sure you will learn things that you never imagined.

It all started one fine morning in early April 1913. I remember it quite clearly. Despite a slight nip in the air, the sun was chasing away the last tendrils of stubborn fog that hovered over London like slow-moving phantoms. In a steady ebb the unwanted specters dissolved, sunlight piercing their opaque bodies until they dissipated, and a vibrant blue sky emerged.

It was my first day at my uncle's accounting firm. That morning I was wearing my favorite new bowler hat and was fastening the buttons on my coat when a plucky little rascal, beckoning to his classmates to wait for him, streaked across my path. He nearly collided with me. Luckily, my impeccable balance saved us both from a terrible spill.

"I say, young man," I admonished him, readjusting my hat. "Slow down."

A tattered book tucked under his arm, the lad spun around, his legs pumping for all they were worth, and he gave me the briefest of glances.

"Sorry, sir!" he shouted, before completing his dizzy rotation and falling into line with the boys who walked several paces ahead of us. "Hey lads, guess what?"

The boys, steadfast in their march toward school, barely acknowledged the younger boy who'd barreled into their midst.

"Guess what?" he repeated. "I told you I was right about Captain Hook!"

A jeering round of laughter broke out among the group. Much too intent on proving his point, the boy ignored the jibe.

"Me dad heard another man talkin' about Hook at the Liar's Pub last night," he said.

"Not that again, Jo-Jo." a dark-haired boy said. "Everybody knows that only bairns and those addle-brained Darlings believe in Captain Hook."

"Mister Barrie believed in him," Jo-Jo said. "He wrote the book about Peter Pan."

"You mean that fairytale he wrote?" The dark-haired boy shook his head. "You're as fuddled as your dad."

Another rousing chorus of laughter broke out among the group, prompting Jo-Jo's footsteps to stall. Head hanging, he fell behind the rowdy band, dragging his boots across the cobblestones. I felt a certain sympathy for Jo-Jo. As a young lad, I had also been ostracized by people because I voiced my fantastical notions. Most of them still thought I was a madman for taking an annual holiday to visit Ireland in search of leprechauns. I haven't found one yet, but I most certainly shall one day.

Jo-Jo's plight, though quite sad, turned out to be a most fortuitous opportunity for me. It seemed almost providential that this high-spirited boy had chosen the same exact route as me to walk to the school. It was a sign that I should change my career from accountant's apprentice to a journalist.

Some of you may think this is rather abrupt. Never fear, dear reader. I'm something of a Renaissance man. My ability to flitter from one job to the next, without any related experience, is renowned in these parts. Yes, I could see it all quite clearly. I, David J. Locke, would seek out Captain Hook, conduct the interview of a lifetime, and become an immediate sensation.

First things first, of course. Before I could begin my investigation, I had to speak with young Master Jo-Jo and discover the whereabouts of the infamous captain.

Fingers itching to transcribe the lad's account, I approached him and I saw that his eyes were glistening with unshed tears. "I say there, Jo-Jo, don't let those hooligans get you down."

"No one ever believes me." He kicked at a loose stone and watched its progression across the street. With a loud clacking sound, the stone bounced off the wheel of a passing bread cart and was lost from sight.

I inhaled the fresh scents of yeast and dough drifting off the cart, and my stomach reminded me that I hadn't eaten yet. I disregarded the sensation and focused on the matter at hand. "I believe you."

Skeptical at first, Jo-Jo's eyes were slow to light up, a small grin plucking at the corners of his mouth. "You do?"

"Of course. You seem like an honest fellow."

Warming to my sincerity, Jo-Jo gave me an eager nod, his grin widening. "Oh, I'm very honest, sir. I'm the only one in the whole class who's never had to do lines for lying to the teacher."

"Splendid." The sun warming us, we resumed our trek toward the school. "So, tell me your story of Captain Hook."

Jo-Jo's eyes turned serious. "It's no story, sir, it's a rumor."

"Quite so. Go on."

"Me dad heard that there was a great hullabaloo at Kensington Gardens the other night. A constable arrested a man, who was running about waving a butterfly net." Jo-Jo proceeded to do a wonderful impersonation of someone swinging a butterfly net while he spoke. "The man was yelling that he was trying to catch fairies for Captain Hook."

My breath lodged in my chest. "Indeed. Did the man say anything else?"

Jo-Jo gave a solemn nod. "He said Hook is alive."

"He survived the crocodile attack?"

"Aye."

"Extraordinary! Did he say where Hook was?"

With a victorious smile, Jo-Jo nodded. "He's living in Madagascar."

For the briefest of moments, I was unsure. Like everyone else, I had read Mister Barrie's account of the Darlings' adventures in Neverland. I had participated in lengthy debates about the book's credibility. How could you not? The excerpt of the poor boy losing his shadow in the nursery was quite convincing. I lose my shadow every single night when the lamps go out.

Of course, I believed that Peter Pan visited small children in our world and lured them to Neverland. The questions nagging at me were: How did Captain Hook survive the crocodile attack? Did the captain really come here or was it an imposter? And finally, why would the captain come here?

If the rumors concerning Hook were true, this could be the biggest opportunity of my aspiring journalistic career: a chance to talk to the old scallywag and end the argument over the truth of Peter Pan's existence. And even more appealing,

I could be the first to write Hook's version of what happened with Peter Pan and the Lost Boys.

I peered down at Jo-Jo and extended my hand in friendship. The school bell rang. "I say, my good little man, you, best get to school. Thank you for passing on the rumor."

"You're welcome, sir." Jo-Jo shook my hand and tore off down the street disappearing into a tidy brick building with the rest of his classmates.

As for me, I promptly made an about face and retraced my steps back the way I'd just come. Kensington Gardens was a few blocks from the stately home I shared with my kind and wealthy grandmother.

With purpose, I strolled into Kensington Gardens, toward The Long Water. An array of flowers lined my path, their soft petals waving to me in the breeze. I admired the neatly trimmed lawns and hearty geraniums guiding my way. Even now as an adult, I often visit the lake while on my way to search for fairies. Ever since my grandmother read me Thomas Tickells's poem *Kensington Gardens*, I've had a fascination with them.

Peter Pan's statue stood on a raised circular dais, close by The Long Water. It is widely believed in these parts that fairies erected the bronze statue one-night last year as a surprise for children. Naturally, I assumed that if there were any sign of recent fairy activity, it would be near Peter Pan's statue. It didn't take me long to find a ripped piece of mesh lining from a butterfly net. From a tree branch bathed in sunlight, the ragged scrap beckoned to me, flapping like a moth stretching its wings before its inaugural flight. I picked up the netting and slipped it into my pocket, a newfound purpose brewing inside me. I knew what I had to do: I would quit my new job at my uncle's accounting firm and prepare for an adventure on the high seas.

Huzzah!

Chapter 2

On a rainy day just a few weeks later, I booked passage on a merchant ship called the *Nevermore*, bid my sweetheart Mable farewell, and set sail for the far-off island of Madagascar. The *Nevermore* was a noisy beast of a ship, bearing a single stack that belched black smoke into the air.

Before departing, I had learned from my uncle that for this journey I would be the sole passenger, and the cargo being transported was not to be discussed. When I asked for details concerning the nature of the cargo, he had none to offer. However, he did give me what he called a sound piece of advice: "Don't meddle, me boy." I reassured him that I was a journalist, not a busybody.

The captain, Captain Crane, was a hearty man and a right charming fellow. Under a jolly blue sky, he greeted me at the gangplank, waving me on board with gusto. " 'Urry up, you, and get on! I ain't got all day."

"Right you are, my good sir." With a spring in my step, I bustled on board. The smell of salt and sea air filling up my lungs, I leaned over the railing, waving one last goodbye to my love. "I'll see you in six months," I called down to her, "and upon my return, we shall be married."

Mable waved her kerchief at me like a flag, then dabbed her hazel eyes with it. Sweet lass. We had met only the week before, but I knew with all my heart that she was my one true love. Both our families insisted that our engagement was a tad precipitous. Codswallop! If you believe, like I, that dragon fire can turn an acorn into a diamond, then love at first sight is a much simpler enterprise.

Soon the anchor was raised and the *Nevermore* slid away from its berth and out of the port, cutting through the waters of the English Channel like a knife through Banoffee Pie. Squinting against the sun, I watched as the port drew farther away for a few seconds, and then I turned around to formally greet the crewmembers nearby.

"Hullo, everyone," I said. When no one answered I called out again, louder this time as I strolled to the center of the deck. "I said, hullo, everyone!"

Taking notice of me, some of the men paused in their quiet, huddled conversations. Others looked up from their seafaring chores to stare at me.

"Good day to you all," I called with a hearty wave.

They didn't reply. They continued to stare at me.

Finally, one undersized sailor threw down his rag, cracked his neck, and looked me over like I was a piece of steak. "Oy, look at this cheerful dolt." He cupped his hands around his mouth and shouted, "Nellie Legs!"

The sailors surrounding him burst into a chorus of chuckles and took up the cry of, "Nellie Legs!"

Being a good sport, I waved them on and chanted, "Nellie Legs," along with them. I still have no idea what Nellie Legs means. I thought perhaps it was a nickname for new members aboard their ship. All in all, I thought it best to play along. I'd never before received such a rousing welcome. It was overwhelming.

Another cheerful crew member, bless him, was so concerned that I might be hungry that he threw an apple at me. The man had a terrible aim, nearly hitting me in the head with it. I picked up the apple and realized that it was rotten to the core. Staring at the apple, I couldn't determine if he was trying to be rude or kind. After a moment's deliberation, my idealistic nature intervened; I decided that he was being kind and thanked him.

I moved to shake this generous sailor's hand, my leather shoes clicking on the wooden decking. With a shrewd eye (he only had one), he watched me, the muscles of his bare arms rippling like the waves in the ocean.

"I say, my good man, what is your name?" I asked.

Towering above his comrades, the sailor crossed his tattooed forearms over his chest, his one eye following my every move. For the briefest of seconds, his stony glare gave me pause. I found myself breaking out in a cold sweat, my feet slowing. I did my best to look upon him with optimistic eyes, but the man still looked quite menacing.

Without warning, a sturdy hand seized my elbow and steered me away from the scene. "Come, Mister Locke," a genteel voice encouraged. "Let's get you to your cabin."

Lightheaded, I dropped the apple, allowing the man to direct me down a short flight of metal stairs and through a dimly lit hallway that was lined with nautical paintings and timber doors bearing bronze numbers. We stopped at number six and he fished around in his pocket.

"This is yours, sir," he said, holding up a key. "You must have forgotten to claim it when you arrived on board."

"Quite so," I agreed, grateful to this well-mannered man for his kindness.

A quick flash of light from an overhead lamp bounced off the key before it disappeared from my sight. I heard him push the key into the keyhole, a telltale clicking sound, and within seconds the door swung open.

The sight of my trunk, safe and sound on the bed, roused me from my fretful daydreaming. I think all of the excitement on deck had overwhelmed me. I wasn't used to being in such a robust company. With a grateful sigh, I sat down beside the trunk and got a good look at my savior.

How should I describe him? He was a spry old man, slightly peaked, long-faced, beardless, and bald. His right arm was in a sling, his sad blue eyes watchful behind his spectacles.

"Thank you, sir, for assisting me," I said. "What is your name?"

The man gave a throaty cough before answering. "Everyone calls me Jimbone."

It was hardly a proper name for such a courteous, altruistic fellow. Perhaps the name was an alias, a necessary nom de plume for a man in hiding. Had I stumbled upon another story that might make my career soar? I was intrigued.

"It's a pleasure to meet you." I stuck out my left hand and he shook it. "You know, Jimbone, I believe that man on deck... What was his name? The giant with one eye?"

"Black-Eyed Bob."

"The men on this ship do have the most colorful names. Well, I don't think Black-Eyed Bob likes me."

"No, you are probably right. Don't take it personally. He doesn't like most people."

Jimbone seemed to be a societal conundrum, a living riddle if you will. How could a man with such well-bred manners, and such a polished way of speaking bear a name like Jimbone?

"Does he like you?"

"Yes."

"Consider yourself lucky. I do believe that if you hadn't intervened he would have hurt me."

"Yes, I believe that you are quite right," Jimbone said.

His matter-of-fact response startled me. It seemed that the men on this boat derived from a much heartier stock than I. Still, Jimbone had come to my assistance, it was a long journey, and I needed a friend. I dug through my trunk for my box of tea.

"I'm grateful to you," I said, opening the box and sniffing the sweet and spicy scent. My mouth watered at the rich aroma. I tilted the box in Jimbone's direction with an encouraging nod. He obliged me and sniffed the tea.

"Wonderful. Do I smell cinnamon and cloves?"

I grinned at his olfactory organ's keen perception. "Indeed it is, Jimbone, my friend, and if you can conjure up a pot of hot water and milk, I will treat you to the best chai tea you've ever had. It's straight from India."

From the gleam in his eye, I could tell that he was tempted.

"Come on, old boy, a spot of tea never hurt anyone," I said.

"Very well," he replied. "Meet me in the dining hall tomorrow morning at six before I start duty."

I was hoping we could have the tea there and then, but I understood that he was a busy man and accepted his offer.

He left whistling a quiet rendition of Mozart's Piano Concerto Number 21. I was so startled by the unexpected melody, I nearly dropped the tea. Fortunately, I was able to steady the tin before it tumbled to the floor, all the while theorizing about Jimbone's upbringing. If the whistled jingle was any indication, he must have rubbed elbows with cultured members of high society. I was determined to discover the truth of his background.

I awoke the next morning feeling dog tired. The sea had been rough during the night, huge waves rocking the ship to and fro like a rose petal in a windstorm, and it had robbed me of a good night's sleep. A good cup of tea was what I needed.

Jimbone!

My hand scrambled at the bedside table for my pocket watch. I hoped I hadn't overslept. I peered at the time and breathed a shaky sigh of relief. It was only 5:30. I threw off my covers and dressed in haste, thinking of the scent of warm cloves and cinnamon. Ten minutes later, I found myself in the dining area, a dingy hall reeking of mildew and burnt coffee. Rough, weathered tables and well-worn benches were set in compact rows, which allowed the crewmen to walk in single file to their seats.

The hall was filled with the buzz of voices as the crew members ate their breakfast and made small talk about the voyage. In a sea of round, black hats, I caught sight of a bald head. Jimbone, a welcome sight, sat alone in a far-off corner. I made my way over to him, careful to avoid Black-Eyed Bob and his mates. A furtive glance to my right told me that they were caught up in an arm-wrestling match and money was being thrown down on the table with much enthusiasm. It seemed the odds were in Black-Eyed Bob's favor. I wouldn't bet against him.

Steering clear of the raucous scene, I bid good morning to Jimbone, who acknowledged me with a curt nod. I sat down across from him, eyeing the steaming teapot, a small pitcher of milk, a cup of sugar, and two cups and saucers, which were set up carefully in front of him.

"I must say, old boy, I appreciate your taking the time to gather up these little extras." I took out my tea leaves and we busied ourselves preparing our drinks.

"I do miss high tea," Jimbone said, stirring milk into his tea.

I thought I also saw him drop a pill into his tea but I coudln't be sure. I've seen my grandmother do it many times with her medicine. She says it's easier to take that way. "We still have it on Saturdays at my grandmother's."

An unruly shout of laughter erupted from the other side of the room and Black-Eyed Bob heaved a bench at the cooks who stood behind a counter. It hit two of the unsuspecting lads in the head, sending them crashing to the floor.

"Bee's knees!" The men surrounding Black-Eyed Bob cheered, and more money was passed around to grunts of pleasure and dismay.

I took a long look at Jimbone as he sipped his tea, the pinky on his left hand extended. "I must say, Jimbone, I can't understand why a man of culture like yourself would want to work on a ship like this."

He gave the room a doleful stare, scrutinizing the boisterous activity surrounding us.

"It's not easy," he replied. "What brings you here?"

Afraid that he'd think me a naive buffoon, I was reluctant to answer. I prided myself on my intellectual and social prowess. It wasn't easy to admit that I had left home on a whim, letting chance chart my course. Normally I was a thoughtful man, methodical in nature and deliberate in my life choices.

"I saw the lass you left behind," Jimbone said. "What could pull a man away from the charms of such beauty?"

I had to be subtle in my answer or risk blowing my chance at being the first to interview the infamous Captain Hook. "I'm off to do the interview of a lifetime in Madagascar."

Interested, Jimbone leaned in, his bum arm sliding across the table and upsetting the sugar cup. "What's in Madagascar?"

"A certain pirate," I said vaguely.

"A certain pirate, eh? There's only one pirate that I've heard of living down there that would drive a seasoned newspaperman from his home..." He let the sentence hang like unfinished laundry in the air.

Unable to contain my excitement, I burst out, "You know about Captain Hook?"

Jimbone clapped his hand over my mouth. "Silence!" he hissed. "Do you want everyone to hear?"

"No," I whispered, pulling back. "How do you know about Captain Hook?"

Behind his spectacles, a storm flared up in Jimbone's eyes. A wry smile tweaked his lips, his neck muscles straining as if he were battling some internal conflict. I swear if he'd had a cutlass he'd have cut the teapot in half.

"Any well-traveled seaman knows about the great Captain James T. Hook." He said the name with relish. It was as if he'd heard it a million-and-one times and was still delighted in the sound of it.

His reaction to the name caught me by surprise. I'd never seen such a contrary display of emotions. I couldn't discern whether he admired or despised the infamous pirate. The journalist in me demanded answers.

As quickly as the storm arose, the darkness passed from his eyes. His shoulders relaxed into the wool of his reefer jacket. Composed, he sipped at his tea and the transformation was so extreme that I began to question whether his earlier reaction had even occurred. I looked around the room, eyeing the sailors.

"Yes, they know of Captain Hook, as well," Jimbone said with an impatient wave of his hand. "It is best not to say his name in their presence."

"Why?"

Another flicker of anger raged across his face, followed by a wan smile. "Let's just say they know enough of his story that hearing his name makes their tempers flare up."

Understandable, I thought. Captain Hook was an evil wretch.

Without warning, Black-Eyed Bob and his mates started a fist fight with another group of sailors from another table. In no time at all, everyone in the hall, apart from Jimbone and I in our little alcove, was caught up in a food fight.

"Don't worry," Jimbone said. "They do this once or twice a week to blow off steam. They won't bother us."

With some trepidation, I followed Jimbone's self-possessed example and did my best to ignore the behavior.

"So, do you know the pirate captain well?" I asked, my voice raised so that I could be heard over the noise that the men were making.

"Of course," Jimbone said, with equal volume. "I've met him."

My jaw dropped, the room falling away around me and the liveliness of the men becoming background noise. I *knew* there was more to Jimbone than he had let on. Proud that my instincts had been spot on, I tried to coax the story of this meeting with Captain Hook out of him. He was reluctant at first, but after much cajoling and the promise of another round of chai tea, he relented.

"How did he survive the crocodile attack?" I asked.

Jimbone seemed pleased with the question. Indeed he was almost giddy with joy, like a child being asked to choose their favorite treat at the bakery. His eyes grew as wide as portholes, his voice shaking with pent-up emotion.

"The crocodile spat him back out," he said, a delighted sparkle in his eye. Jimbone smiled when he saw the look of astonishment on my face.

"Impossible!" I gasped.

Jimbone glowered at me. "Nothing's impossible."

A horn blasted, causing me to jump, and Jimbone released me from his stony glare. In unison, all the men around us stopped their destructive activity, as if a referee had called a cordial end to a game of rugger. With genial affection, they clapped each other on the backs and began exiting the hall to begin their daily nautical duties. They ambled through the double doors, bidding Captain Crane, who had suddenly materialized, a good morning.

As stoic as any ship's mast, the captain stood chewing on the stump of a pipe, the whites of his eyes as prominent as an ivory sail shining in the sun. The captain was quite unlike the man I had met on deck yesterday. His ruddy complexion had faded and his bluster had blown itself out. He stared hard at Jimbone and me, and it felt as if he were trying to use his glare alone to summon Jimbone's attention. Quite unperturbed, Jimbone didn't move. He gave the captain a perfunctory glance, then sipped at his tea, seemingly content to sit there all day and debate the truth of his outlandish story about Captain Hook.

Once again I peered over my shoulder. My anxiety mounted. Captain Crane was still in the doorway.

"Why is the captain staring at us?" I whispered to my companion.

Jimbone shrugged. "He must have a question for me. He may be the captain of this ship, but I'm the one who makes the decisions."

"I'm afraid I don't understand."

"The crew answers to him and he answers to me."

I was befuddled by this new information. How could Jimbone be in charge? Why was there such intrigue on a merchant ship?

Jimbone grinned at my confusion. "Do you like a good mystery, Mister Locke?"

"Doesn't everyone?"

With a hearty chuckle, Jimbone straightened his spectacles and motioned for Captain Crane to join us. Proving who was truly in charge of the vessel, the captain immediately obeyed Jimbone and sat down beside me. He sat upright, his arms folded and resting on the table, fingers tapping across his forearm in agitation.

"Good morning, Captain Crane," I said. "Are you unwell?"

He replied with a throaty grunt, his undivided attention focused on Jimbone.

"Report," Jimbone said.

"We are on schedule and the..." Captain Crane gave me a cautionary glance and paused, unsure if he should continue with his briefing.

Jimbone waved his teacup at me in a lazy fashion. "This one's all right. You may continue."

Captain Crane cleared his throat and shifted uncomfortably in his seat. "The cargo," he whispered, leaning across the table, "is becoming—unstable."

Unstable? I gave Captain Crane a pointed look.

Jimbone sat at ease, stirring milk into his tea. "I told you not to go near the cargo," he said, a touch of menace creeping into his voice.

Captain Crane turned the color of a pale mushroom.

"What exactly is it doing?" Jimbone asked.

After giving a cursory glance around the empty hall, Captain Crane leaned in so close to Jimbone that his chest was on the table. He whispered into the bald man's ear, a look of astonished disbelief on his face.

"It's floating," he said.

Floating? Had I heard correctly?

"Is it?" Jimbone asked, a smile on his lips. He seemed to be enjoying a private joke.

"Is there a leak on the ship?" I asked.

"Not a drop 'o water anywhere," Captain Crane said. "I checked it meself three times."

He cowered under the glare Jimbone shot him. Clearly, the old man was displeased that Captain Crane had not left the cargo alone.

I wanted to question the captain further, but hesitated when I saw the expression on Jimbone's face, unable to discern if he wanted to throw Captain Crane overboard or offer him a cup of tea to soothe his nerves. I thought it wise to remain silent. The fluctuation in Jimbone's mood confused me. He wasn't alarmed by the captain's declaration in the slightest, only irked that he'd disobeyed his orders. Either something strange was afoot or Captain Crane had suffered a hallucination. Cargo could not float if it was not in water, surely.

Jimbone took a long sip of tea, giving Captain Crane time to try and recover his wits. The man had expected Jimbone to be shocked at the news, and the fact that he was not in the least bit out of countenance clearly disturbed the captain a great deal. An expression of utter confusion washed over the captain's face. He muttered to himself for a good while, his lips twitching like a field mouse's nose. After much incoherent deliberation, the confounded look in his eyes receded and a skeptical expression took over. It seemed he didn't know what to think and his guard was up.

I was also unsure of what to think. Obviously, the captain was rattled. Perhaps he was losing his mind. I felt relieved knowing that Jimbone was in charge. As a well-grounded man who is firmly rooted in reality, it's easy for me to spot a balanced fellow with good common sense. I reckoned if Jimbone wasn't worried about the cargo, I shouldn't be worried about it either.

"There, there, Captain Crane. Why don't you have some tea?" Jimbone asked.

Swearing under his breath, Captain Crane reclaimed his seat beside me, looking me over like I was the one who was losing his mind. He withdrew a flask from his pocket and took a swig. After giving a satisfied belch, he turned to us and asked, "What were you two talkin' about earlier?"

"This one here is on his way to see Captain Hook," Jimbone said.

In the midst of another swallow from his flask, Captain Crane choked, sputtered, and thumped his chest. Upon recovering from his coughing fit, he gave me a long, disbelieving stare.

"Are you thick in the head?" he rasped, with a half-reproving glance at Jimbone, "There ain't no such thing as Captain Hook!"

"Indeed there is, sir," I argued, expecting Jimbone to support my claim.

Captain Crane chortled. "Your uncle told me you were a bit daft. Next, you'll tell us you believe in fairies and flying boys from Neverland."

Feeling as defensive as Jo-Jo, I answered, "I do."

Captain Crane threw a knowing glance in Jimbone's direction. "Completely off his rocker!" he howled, slapping his knee.

"He is a bit naive," Jimbone agreed, with a wink in my direction, "but you're the one who is seeing things floating about the ship."

A startled look crossed the captain's face. It was clear that he didn't appreciate Jimbone's innuendo that he was crazy. He made the sign against evil and pushed away from the table, rising unsteadily to his feet.

"I'll be on me way," he grunted.

As soon as the captain was out of earshot, Jimbone laughed.

"So, you don't believe the captain saw floating cargo?" I asked.

Jimbone gave a non-committal shrug. "Do you?"

"I don't consider myself a Doubting Thomas, but I think I'd need to see the cargo for myself before I decided."

"A splendid idea," Jimbone announced, rising at once. "Let's inspect it for ourselves."

Without waiting to see if I were following him, he marched off toward the door, pushing it open with a flourish and sweeping through before it swung back. Abandoning my tea, I hastened after him, not knowing what to expect, but hoping against hope that the cargo was as bewitched as the captain had claimed. I knew sailors were a superstitious lot. If rumors of a haunted cargo spread across the ship, panic would abound. There could be a mutiny! Oh, but what a splendid addition to my article such drama would be.

Chapter 3

Jimbone and I trooped along the empty corridors. The rest of the men were either working on deck or in the bowels of the ship, making our passage through the hallways easy and uneventful. Every now and then we'd pass a sailor who'd spare us a sidelong glance or a silent scowl, but other than that, no one questioned us. We made our way down several twisting staircases, the light growing murkier with every level that we descended. The noise of our booted feet was muted against the ship's constant discordant clamoring.

Jimbone opened one door and somewhere in the distance, I heard the raised voices of men as they spoke over the roaring engine and hissing pipes. At the bottom of the next set of stairs, the path split into two: a catwalk veered off to the left toward the engine room and a set of steps plunged further into the bowels of the ship.

We took the stairs, walking cautiously as the darkness closed in around us. When we came to the next corridor, the only source of light was up ahead, where a dim yellow glow outlined a thick metal door. The glow barely gave me enough light to see my feet, but it did serve as a guide to our apparent destination. I could hear a faint tinkling sound from behind the metal door.

"What is that noise?" I asked, the tinkling growing louder with each step we took toward the strange light.

"You'll see soon enough," Jimbone replied, giving the door a good push.

The door swung open with a resounding crash as it hit the wall and bits of rusty debris rained down on us. For a moment, I saw some crates in the middle of the room that were illuminated from within by a buttery light. Then the light went out and we were plunged into darkness. Once the echo of the crash ceased, I noticed that the tinkling sound had stopped, leaving behind a hollow silence that made my ears ring.

"Jimbone," I whispered into the darkness, the tiny hairs on the back of my neck prickling. "What is this?"

"Do not distress yourself, good sir. There's nothing to fear here."

To my right, I heard his footsteps heading toward the crates in the middle of the room. In the utter blackness, I followed the soft thud of his boots.

"Shhh," Jimbone whispered, causing me to halt where I stood. "If we're quiet long enough, they'll light up again."

As we were the only two people in the room, I was confused. "Who?"

"The fairies."

"Fairies?" I ventured, my voice echoing around the room like a bell tolling the hour.

"I told you to be quiet," Jimbone growled, seizing my jacket sleeve and giving me such a shake that my teeth fair rattled. He released me and a moment later an oil lamp flared to life in his hand, sending out a halo of light that surrounded us like a bubble. Under the pale ring of light, his cheeks were gaunt, his eyes swallowed up in shadow, which gave him the look of a hollow-eyed skull.

My mouth went dry at the sight of him, my tongue sticking to the roof of it like an over baked biscuit. I had half a mind to flee until the light within one crate re-ignited and I could hear a soft, desperate tinkling sound. In a single bound, Jimbone discarded his lamp and was upon the crate, his left hand splayed across its surface, speaking into a slatted opening.

"Tink!" he cried, as darkness overtook the crate again. He banged on the lid. "Please listen to me."

He turned to me, the murky glow from the lamp providing inadequate light to get the true measure of his expression, but the anguish in his voice was unmistakable.

"I've been trying for days," he wailed, "but she won't talk to me."

Horror grew inside me as I began to comprehend what was unfolding before my eyes. "Is there a real live fairy in there?"

Sagging against the crate, Jimbone nodded and sniffled, his right elbow perched on the crate to support his weight. During his outburst, his sling had shifted, allowing his right arm to escape its confinement. I couldn't be sure in the semi-darkness, but his right arm appeared to be slightly shorter than his left. How odd.

"Yes," Jimbone said. "It's Tinker Bell, my oldest and dearest friend."

My heart plummeted, dragging my stomach along with it to my ankles. I am a brave man, but this revelation tested my resolve.

What would Peter Pan and the Lost Boys do when they found out Jimbone had taken Tinker Bell? Would they want revenge against me, an unwilling accomplice, as well? According to all accounts, Peter Pan was impulsive and had violent tendencies. He was a cunning and capable warrior. As a young boy, he fought Captain Hook, a grown man, in combat and cut off the captain's right hand with a single blow of his knife. Being an impetuous fellow, Peter may not realize that I had no part in this scheme.

My gaze fell upon Jimbone's right arm again, surveying its awkward appearance. Through the gloom, my eyes could discern what they had failed to recognize earlier: where a hand should reside, there was only a stump.

"What happened to your right hand?" I asked.

Jimbone flinched and looked morosely at his right arm. "That wretched boy Peter Pan cut it off and fed it to the crocodile."

"How barbaric."

"Indeed," Jimbone said.

"How many hands has he cut from people's bodies?" I asked, flexing all ten of my fingers and cherishing the feel of each digit.

"Only one."

"But I thought he had cut off Captain Hook's hand. How...?"

"You simple-minded fool. I am Captain Hook!" Jimbone bellowed. "But I'm not supposed to be Captain Hook anymore. It's Peter's turn. He broke the rules of the game. If only Tink would talk to me. There must be a way she can help. She alone has the ability to change Peter's mind when he is set on a certain course."

Hands trembling, I fumbled for the hanky in my pocket and wiped the nervous sweat from my face and neck. I tried to determine how to deal with the situation, without upsetting the man further. "P-perhaps if you let her out of the crate, she'll feel more inclined to talk."

"She'll fly away if I do that," he growled as if that were obvious.

"Fly away?" How far could she get in this dingy room that had but one door and no windows?

"I've been collecting fairies for some time now. I need them and their fairy dust to get back to Neverland. And I need answers," he said, motioning to the six other crates. They were stacked in columns of three, adjacent to the solitary one that contained Tink. "It's taken me years to get her back."

His desolation evaporating, he pushed away from Tink's crate with renewed zeal, as if some new, mad purpose had taken hold of him. He grabbed my elbow and ushered me closer to the crate. "That's why I brought you down here. You must talk to her," he insisted, prodding me in the back. "Help her to understand."

"Understand what?"

"Why I needed to kidnap her."

I felt faint all over again. I wanted no part in this treachery. Kidnapping fairies and locking them away in crates like animals was intolerable, but I could see no way out of the situation, so I crouched down beside the crate. "What would you like me to say?"

Now that I was cooperating, the frenzied look in his eyes had abated. He pulled himself up tall and focused on the task at hand. "Tell her it was his turn to be the pirate and she knows it."

I'm sure Tinker Bell heard every word he'd shouted. Dumbfounded, I relayed the message anyway. Absolute silence was the only response I received.

"Tell her I'm desperate," Jimbone seethed.

"Please, Miss Bell," I said, "he's desperate."

Still no reply. Finally, my curiosity got the better of me. I needed to know what the captain had been referring to when he'd claimed it wasn't his turn to be Captain Hook anymore. I cleared my throat. "Captain Hook?"

"Don't call me that!" Jimbone snarled. "I have been Captain Hook long enough."

"I'm afraid I don't understand. What exactly do you mean by that?"

Impatient and weary, Jimbone sighed. "Peter Pan and James Hook are characters that another boy and I made up. It started out as a game, Peter Pan and the Lost Boys against Captain Hook and the pirates."

"What happened?"

"The other boy and I would take turns being Peter Pan and Captain Hook, and our friends would also switch being the Lost Boys and the pirates."

"Who was this other boy?"

"James Peter. Tinker Bell conveyed us to Neverland at about the same time. James Peter arrived a few days before me. When James Peter and I discovered that our names were almost identical, we thought it was brilliant."

"Almost identical?"

"My name is Peter James. James Peter and I were very much alike in appearance and voice. Tink always said we could have been twins. We became instant friends, played the best games, and had the greatest adventures until..."

The joyful nostalgia in his voice turned bitter, trailing off on a dark note. He was quiet for a while. I hoped he would continue with his tale, but I was reluctant to ask him to elaborate. His hostility was so tangible, it filled up the darkness. After a period of dour silence, Hook continued his story.

"I was the first one to play Peter Pan," he said, "and he was the first to play Captain James T. Hook."

"I've always wondered, what does the T stand for?"

Hook heaved a great sigh. "The T stands for tyrant. Oh, we thought we were so clever, but then we began to notice changes."

"What type of changes?" I asked.

"Whenever it was time for the one playing Captain Hook to take their turn, they aged. The last time we played the game, James Peter refused to switch places with me. So I was stuck as Hook and I grew up."

"Why didn't you just stop playing?"

"Because it was part of the game. The rule was that only Peter Pan had the power to end the game and James Peter didn't want to stop playing. Or rather he did not want to play the part of Captain Hook. He wanted to be Peter Pan forever. Selfish, cocky boy, forcing me to play the game and remain Captain Hook!"

"That's terrible! Why did you give Peter Pan total control of the game?"

Jimbone sighed again. "It was my idea. The worst one I've ever had. We had pretended Hook was a grown-up for the game because all pirates are grown-ups. We knew all grown-ups were bossy. I didn't want Hook and the pirates thinking they could tell Peter Pan and the Lost Boys what to do, so I suggested that Peter Pan should have power over everything, especially the grown-ups. James Peter agreed and took advantage of that rule when it was time to switch places."

"That was very unfair."

"Yes, very bad form, indeed." He held his right arm up high. "After Peter Pan cut off my hand that blasted crocodile hunted me down, finally swallowing me whole." He shuddered. "But, since I had been the original Peter Pan, I still had some leverage over the beast. Neverland will not let Peter Pan die, even a second-rate one."

"Why not?"

"Because Peter Pan was the spark of life Neverland needed. I may have been playing someone else, but I was the first Peter Pan. The crocodile could sense this and so it spat me out." He paused to suck in a breath. "I retreated the moment I was free of that beast. Tinker Bell found me sometime later and banished me from Neverland. Naturally, I refused to leave. When my pirates, the loyal mates that they are, heard

I was still alive, they joined me on my ship. One night, while we slept, we were taken away from Neverland together. We've been trying to find a way back ever since."

"Why were you banished?"

"Due to the nature of the game we'd designed, James Peter and I would have no choice but to continue fighting forever and the fairies couldn't allow this."

"Why would it go on forever?"

"Because we'd made Pan and Hook equally formidable. The only way to end it was to separate us permanently. So, the fairies did the only thing they could: they helped Neverland banish me."

He breathed another sigh, his voice laden with remorse and loneliness. "How I miss the rivalry, the battles. We had the greatest adventures."

Shoulders curved in defeat, his melancholy filled up the silence. Eyeing the dispirited old pirate, I couldn't help feeling sorry for Jimbone.

"How did Tinker Bell manage to banish you?"

Jimbone's mouth turned down, his voice grim. "Since I refused to leave, she and some of her fairy friends waited until my men and I were asleep aboard our ship and flew us out."

I surveyed the crates stacked around me. "How many fairies have you captured?"

"Two hundred and eighty-seven."

"They should give you more than enough fairy dust to fly back to Neverland."

"That's true. But I've been banished. The only way a human can get into Neverland is with a fairy escort."

"Why won't they escort you?"

"Because they are loyal to Peter Pan."

"How can you get them to be loyal to you again?"

"I don't know." He banged a fist on Tinker Bell's crate. "That's why I need to talk to her."

A furious jangling noise erupted from inside the crate. Afraid she may smash the crate with her fairy rage, I leapt away from it. "What did she say?"

Jimbone grinned. "She insulted me for kidnapping her!" he cried with delight. He ran back to the crate and pressed his mouth to a slat. "Oh, Tink. I've missed you."

She replied with more angry chatter.

Jimbone laughed aloud, his eyes twinkling. "Will you help me then?" he asked Tinker Bell.

Another wave of furious jangling erupted from inside the crate. When it gave a violent shudder and bounced, I drew back even further from it.

"What did she say now?" I asked.

"She never knew that James Peter and I switched places as part of the game. She thought that we had chosen only one role to play." Jimbone grew thoughtful for a second, his eyes focusing on a memory from long ago. After a time, a sad smile moved across his lips. "I guess we forgot to tell her. Since James Peter and I were nearly identical in every way, our ruse worked."

Tinker Bell's volatile outbursts sent splinters through the wood of her crate. Tiny wooden shards sprang up all over the crate like the quills on a porcupine.

"Perhaps you should let her out before the crate explodes?"

All of the fairies jingled and jangled in agreement with me.

Jimbone was reluctant, but I sensed his resolve was breaking. Stroking his stump, he stared at the crates, his eyes filled with a desperate longing. It was obvious he wanted to be reunited with his old friends.

"Come on, old boy," I said. "If you free her, she may listen to you."

After much convincing, Jimbone agreed to let the fairies out of their crates. In no time at all, their rich light and animated chatter filled up the entire room, chasing away the dank gloom. It was a welcome improvement, like the sun appearing in the sky after a long absence and wind chimes stirring in a gentle breeze. The fairies couldn't stay still for very long when they were awake, so it was like watching stars dash about, creating constellation clusters that gilded the air like fireworks.

The fairies were very skeptical of Jimbone at first. Like Tinker Bell, no one knew about the bargain the two boys had made about switching roles. It took Jimbone some time to convince Tink that he was one of two Peter Pans and that he was the original one. When she was finally convinced, she pinched Jimbone on the arm, angry that she had been left out of such a delicious secret. Then she pinched both of his ears. One for each Peter who had tricked her.

With good humor, Jimbone took Tink's abuse. Indeed, he seemed to relish it, as if recapturing a happy moment in time.

"So, you believe me then?" he asked, rubbing his ears.

Tink made a jingling sound.

Jimbone looked at me, a childlike delight all over his face. "She believes me! I want to go home, Tink," he pleaded. "I'm so sick of this game. I just want to be Peter James again."

Tinker Bell explained something to him and he was quiet for a long time. The other fairies gathered around him, their wings, upright, flush with light, and fluttering moments ago, were now dim, their tiny shoulders stooped with sadness.

"That's not fair. I don't want to be a grown-up anymore," he said.

"What did she say?" I asked.

"That it's impossible for me to be a boy again because I've been a grown up for too long."

Defeated, he crumpled to the floor. The dreadful news seemed to overwhelm him. He sunk ever deeper into his coat and exhaled a whimper that twisted and turned into a bitter wail. The wail, laden with decades of heartache, hung in the air and clung to my skin like sweat. Jimbone started sobbing. With a soothing jingle, Tinker Bell perched on the bony protrusion of his shoulder until finally, the heartbroken pirate cried himself to sleep.

He seemed so small curled up on the cold floor. Reluctant to disturb his reprieve from the dreadful truth, the fairies and I watched him sleep for a bit. In silence, they hovered above Jimbone, glittery sentinels watching over their old and greatest playmate.

After a time, I noticed his coloring began to fail under the fairy's light. His eyes were rimmed with gray, his cheeks the sallow color of spoiled milk. Fearful that he had fallen ill, I approached him.

"We should wake him. Jimbone," I said crouching down and trying to rouse him with a shake. "Jimbone!" He did not respond. I peered up at the fairies, hovering over us like a flock of luminescent birds. "Something is amiss."

In a flash, Tinker Bell swooped lower, erratic, a desperate twitter on her lips. She tweaked his nose and pinched his cheeks, her voice escalating, cajoling him to wake up. With a harsh chirping sound, she pulled away from him and began showering him in fairy dust.

The other fairies joined her, covering Jimbone in their magic dust as well. They used their wands to levitate him and, in a procession, we left the cargo room and made our way back to the upper decks. With their combined light, it was easier to find our way. As we neared Jimbone's quarters, Black-Eyed Bob discovered us. His eye widened at the sight of the fairies and Jimbone lying prone in midair.

"What happened?" he asked.

I told him everything that had taken place below.

"Let's get him to his room and I'll fetch Dr. Smeech. Follow me," the big fellow said.

Once Jimbone was settled in bed, Dr. Smeech assessed him. After his examination, the doctor approached us with a grave expression.

"He didn't want me to tell you, Black-Eyed Bob, but he's been sick for a while now," he said. "I fear that Tinker Bell's news about him being unable to become a boy again broke his heart. I doubt he'll recover."

"Aye," Black-Eyed Bob said, nodding. His big, wide face puckered up tight and he hung his head low. "I knew. I saw him clutchin' at his side when he thought no one was lookin', and I saw the medicine on his table that you gave him, Doc." Staring at his ailing friend, he backed out of the room, muttering, "I'll tell the crew."

Over the next few days, Jimbone's condition worsened. He seemed to shrink before our eyes as if some strange beast was eating away at him, stealing the fat from his bones. We tried feeding him a simple broth, but he lost the ability to swallow. Shortly after this, his breathing became labored. After two days of extremely high fevers and fitful sleep, he didn't wake again.

Although the crew drifted in and out of Jimbone's room for updates on his condition, Tinker Bell kept a constant vigil at his bedside, chirping the loveliest of lullabies that wound tendrils of hope and love through the air. Each man who left the room wiped a teary eye, often lingering in the hall for a few moments as if caught in the sweet-sounding web the melody had spun. No mother could have sung more beautifully.

Three days after our journey to the hold, Jimbone died. As the last rays of the sun sank beneath the horizon, his breathing simply stopped. The grimace of pain and illness he'd born for days softened, an expression of peace taking its place. It was a sad day to be sure but a bittersweet one as well. Captain Hook was finally free of Peter Pan's treacherous betrayal. Peter James's part in the harsh Neverland game was forever complete.

As the crew and fairies grieved the loss of their true captain, I roamed about the ship offering condolences and chai tea. When the last of my tea leaves were gone, I returned to my room and started composing this story. After writing a few sentences I found the exercise tiresome and fell asleep.

I awoke later that night. Unable to fall back to sleep, I went on deck for a bit of fresh air. The *Nevermore* was sailing somewhere across the Mediterranean Sea. Good fortune had allowed us to make our journey without the threat of major storms. This night was no exception. All around me the black waters swayed to and fro in gentle waves. The air was cool, settling on my skin like a silk robe. I breathed it in enjoying the quiet solitude of the moment as the world slept.

While the inhabitants of the land slumbered, those that dwelt in the night sky were awake. A dome of the truest midnight blue covered the sea, the stars alive with glittering light. The moon, winking in silver fragments across the sea, was the brightest I had ever seen. Its pearly light bathed the boat, transforming the dull exterior, washing the weatherworn steel until it glowed like polished glass.

As I admired the glittering planks and rails, I saw the ghost of a young boy walking about the ship. Astonished, I blinked, hoping to clear my vision. I thought my eyes were deceiving me, a phantom trick of the light. But, as the boy continued to move I knew that he was real. He was as white as the moonlight but more vivid, outlined in a silvery halo. He looked about in bemused confusion as if he'd just awoken from a long sleep and found himself in some familiar memory.

At his appearance, the stars twinkling merrily above, pulsed and brightened, calling to him in a musical language. *Peter! Peter!*

The song brought the hint of a smile to his lips. He peered up at the stars, thrust out his chin, and crowed to them in a delightful response.

The sound shot straight up and rippled across the dark sky like a tidal wave, awakening even more celestial lights from their slumber until every star in the heavens smiled down on him. One, far off in the distance to the right, shone the brightest of all.

"Peter!" they sang again.

A shadow moved swiftly across the face of the moon. For the briefest of seconds, the shadow vanished, before reappearing in a sudden, fluid motion. The ghostly boy watched the shadow as it ascended the side of the ship and hovered slightly above him. Now under the full light of the moon, the shadow revealed a slim boy dressed in skeleton leaves. Despite one being solid and the other ethereal, the two boys were strikingly similar in appearance, radiating energy and arrogance in equal parts.

The sight was almost eerie. It left me breathless with sadness.

After sizing each other up, the two boys greeted each other.

"Peter Pan," Peter James said. "After all this time we meet again."

Peter Pan grinned.

Peter James didn't return the smile. "I thought you were my friend," he said. "But I was wrong."

"I was your friend," Peter Pan said. "Until you started to grow up."

"I hated you for a long, long time for that. You're a liar and a cheat. But, growing up taught me one thing that you'll never understand."

"What's that?" Peter Pan asked, intrigued by the challenge.

"How to forgive a child for their selfishness."

Peter Pan stared at Peter James then laughed in a careless and carefree way. It was clear he hadn't comprehended the meaning of Peter James's statement. After an immeasurable silence Peter James asked, "Why are you here?"

"I'm here to take you part of the way, Peter James," Peter Pan said.

"The way to where?" Peter James asked.

"The Summer Land," Peter Pan replied.

"Oh, that's right. I remember I used to help children get there, too. I'll never grow up there again, will I?"

"Never, ever."

The boy dressed in leaves raised his chin toward the stars and cried out, "Tinker Bell!"

In a flash of golden, glittering light, Tinker Bell and the other fairies joined the two boys painting a silver bubble around the pair. Instead of taking up her spot beside Peter Pan, Tinker Bell hovered close to Peter James.

"Tink," he said jubilant. "Will you fly beside me the whole way to the Summer Land?"

Tink twittered a response. A ripple of surpirse circled around the group and Peter Pan cried out, "You can't go to the Summer Land with him! You're my fairy!"

She responded with another high-pitched chrip and drew even closer to Peter James, issuing a softer tone in his direction.

"She's right," Peter James said. "She can go wherever she wants and..." He looked at her with wide eyes. "Do you really mean that last part about being my fairy first?"

Tink nodded.

For a moment Peter Pan looked forlorn, his voice full of the innocence of a brokenhearted child as he asked,"Will you visit me in Neverland sometimes, Tink?"

Tink chirped a reply that brought a small smile to Peter Pan's face.

"It's settled then," Peter Pan said.

Both Peters gazed upward and together the happy group flew off toward the stars. My heart swelling with emotion, I dabbed my eyes and watched them until they disappeared into the night. I was sorry that Jimbone had died, but found solace knowing he'd been reunited with Tinker Bell and was able to reconcile with her and Peter Pan. The fearsome pirate would finally find the eternal youth he longed for, in the Summerland.

Chapter 4

Following Jimbone's death, Captain Crane locked himself up in the brig until we could return him to shore. A superstitious man, he thought the crew and I were cursed and wanted to stay as far away from us as possible. The rest of us buried Jimbone's body at sea. The sky that day was a mournful gray as the sea swallowed his body whole. We watched as his face, drawn thin from illness and death, disappeared into the water's dark depths. The only trace that Jimbone had lived were the stories the crewmen shared.

The funeral was a somber affair and a lot of big, burly men cried. They dabbed their eyes and blew their noses in hankies and on shirt sleeves. My arms were sopping wet by the time the funeral was over. The men had taken a liking to my crisp linen shirt. They said it was absorbent.

As for my part, I felt as if I'd been baptized as an honorary pirate from Neverland. I peeled the shirt off the first chance I got and tucked it away in my trunk for safe keeping.

It's not every day that one is christened in the tears of Lost Boys who've been banished from Neverland. What a marvelous experience!

On a more positive note, my staunch loyalty to Jimbone and the men, in their hour of grief, earned me a place among the crew. Despite the sadness of Jimbone's passing, it was an exciting time for me. I became the first mate to Captain Black-Eyed Bob and learned how to navigate using the stars and the ship's compass.

Still mourning the loss of Jimbone, the men longed for their adopted island home of Madagascar. The idea of returning home seemed to lift Black-Eyed Bob's spirits. After a few weeks of quiet travel, we found ourselves in the Indian Ocean. We made berth at a remote seaport in Diego Suarez in northern Madagascar. The view was breathtaking. My eyes drank in the turquoise waters, the white sandy beaches, and the *Pain de Sucre* mountain island. It left me feeling inspired to become a painter, for I had certainly found my muse in the landscape.

I must say, the *Nevermore* was quite conspicuous, being the biggest ship in the port. The locals, in their smaller boats, must have grown used to the presence of the large ship, because they hardly gave us a second glance. A few sailors waved to Black-Eyed Bob and shouted greetings in French. I was delighted to hear the language. I am fluent in five languages, French being one of them. It seemed I would have no trouble speaking with the people here. I was surprised when Black-Eyed Bob returned the salutation and commented about the beautiful weather.

"You know how to speak French?" I asked.

"Of course," Black-Eyed Bob replied, "We all do. We've lived here for many years."

"Quite right, old boy," I said.

Most of the men, craving a warm bed on land, had agreed to a month-long shore leave. Bags slung across their shoulders, they bid us farewell and departed straight away. Disheveled and weary, Captain Crane stomped off of the ship and left us as fast as his legs could carry him, muttering oaths and swearing to take the first ship back to England.

"A pleasure sailing with you, Captain," I called after him.

He kept steady on his course away from us and did not grace me with a reply.

Restless and wanting to stretch our sea legs, Black-Eyed Bob and I went ashore. Under a sunlit sky, we walked among the food stalls and clothing merchants in the market square. My stomach rumbled at the scents of freshly baked bread and spiced meats.

There was a nice crowd of people milling about. Men and women conducted their business with the merchants. Children laughed at the sight of a stray dog dancing on its hind legs, begging for a scrap of meat. Black-Eyed Bob and I stopped at a produce stall to buy some fruit when I noticed a darkly clad man enter the square. His appearance caused many others to pause and stare. A rippling of hushed voices soon surrounded us.

"It's Señor Hector Madrid," they chorused in fear.

"Who is Señor Hector Madrid?" I asked.

A bald man sporting a chinstrap beard eyed me as if I were mad. "He's only the second greatest werewolf hunter in the world," he whispered. His voice held a reverence one assumes when one is speaking in church.

More quiet pleas were uttered from the crowd. "Why is he here alone?", "Where is his partner?" "Was she killed by a werewolf?" "Is there a werewolf among us?"

I peered up at Black-Eyed Bob, who shrugged. He knew as much about Señor Hector Madrid as I did. But his eyes shone with an interest that mirrored my own. My heart rattled in my chest.

Awestruck, people withdrew from Señor Hector Madrid, gawking at him as if he were a king. With long, sure-footed strides, Hector marched passed, nodding his black, broad-brimmed hat at them, as if he were accustomed to this sort of wonderstruck welcome. As the crowd parted, I was able to get a better look at him.

Hector was a stout, barrel-chested man, with long black hair and an impressive handlebar mustache. A small, curved sword hung from one hip and a silver-handled revolver was holstered at the other. Hector came to stand in the very center of the square, his small black eyes skimming over the crowd, freezing them in their tracks.

"Good people," he said, clasping the folds of his vest. "I'm sure you all know who I am."

The crowd replied with restrained acknowledgment. They were not happy that he was there among them.

"I know my appearance has startled some of you. For that I am sorry, but nonetheless, I am looking for volunteers to help me find a werewolf."

A murmur of dissent went up from the crowd. They wanted no part in hunting down a werewolf. Mothers and fathers gathered up their children and scurried from the marketplace. Men and women dropped out of sight through alleyways and wooden doors. The vendors left their wares behind and retreated. Within minutes, the entire square was empty. Only Señor Hector Madrid, Black-Eyed Bob, and I remained.

Hector watched us, his mustache lilting above his half-smile. "Good day to you, gentlemen," he said marching toward us.

Black-Eyed Bob nodded at him.

"It's grand to meet you, sir," I said.

Hector gave Black-Eyed Bob an approving nod in return. His expression soured a bit when he looked at me, but he seemed resigned to accept any help he could get.

"Can I count on the both of you to help me?"

"Of course," I replied, "Apprehending a werewolf…"

Black-Eyed Bob shushed me and spoke to Hector. "What does this sort of job pay?"

"Excellent question," I said, sorry I hadn't thought of that.

Hector chuckled. "The mayor has promised me and my partner one-hundred gold pieces, upon the capture of the werewolf." He squinted and made an odd clicking noise with his tongue. "We'll give you twenty percent of the purse."

Black-Eyed Bob gave Hector a shrewd look. "Twenty percent a piece."

Hector deliberated for a moment and extended his hand. "Agreed."

Satisfied, the two men shook hands.

"Brilliant," I said. "When do we start?"

Hector turned on his booted heel, his cape swishing around his knees. "Come with me."

Hector led us out of the market toward a hill some distance away. The dirt road we followed forked off into three separate routes, two had signs that were so weatherworn I couldn't read them. We took the third route, which had no sign. The dirt path quickly turned into a footpath that snaked its way up the hill. At the top, there was a small campsite, where three horses grazed at leisure and a young woman garbed in a red hooded cloak, sat stoking a fire. She was young, no older than fourteen.

Hector waved a hand toward the girl. "Gentlemen, may I introduce my partner, Little Red, the greatest werewolf hunter in the world."

Little Red pulled back her hood and flashed us a wolfish smile. I knew right then that this was going to be another splendid adventure. After all, I had always wanted to be a werewolf hunter.

About the Author

Ellwyn Autumn is an American author/blogger/ghostwriter and a certified teacher with a Master's Degree in Education. She writes children's picture books, middle-grade novels, and Young Adult fiction. Ellwyn's first self-published novel, Chris Kringle's Cops The First Mission, was a Finalist in the 2016 Reader's Favorite International Book Contest. Her Kamyla Chung picture book series addresses difficult issues facing young children. Kamyla Chung and the Classroom Bully is on Jedlie's Certified Great Reads List and earned Story Monster Approval.

Ellwyn discovered her passion for writing in second grade when she had to write a book report for school. She was so excited to write the report, until her mother told her that she had to write about someone else's book and not her own story. Ellwyn became indignant and decided that once she finished the book report she would most certainly write her own original story. She has been writing ever since!

Ellwyn lives with her family in Pennsylvania. She loves all things magical, curling up with a good book, writing stories, and almost anything with chocolate in it.

https://www.ellwynautumn.com

lemondropliterary.blogspot.com

Printed in Poland
by Amazon Fulfillment
Poland Sp. z o.o., Wrocław